A NORTH-SOUTH PAPERBACK

Critical praise for

A Mouse in the House!

"High-spirited. . . . The story races along . . . providing readers with a real sense of accomplishment when they've turned the last page. The details of dialogue and action bring each character to life, including Socks and Lisa. The scenes have a domestic warmth, juxtaposing the children's exuberance with Mother's exasperation in a way that is both authentic and gently humorous." *Kirkus*

A Mouse in the House!

By Gerda Wagener
Illustrated by Uli Waas

Translated by Rosemary Lanning

North-South Books

NEW YORK · LONDON

Copyright © 1995 by Nord-Süd Verlag AG, Gossau Zürich, Switzerland.
First published in Switzerland under the title *Fetzer jagt die Maus*
English translation copyright © 1995 by North-South Books Inc.

All rights reserved. No part of this book may be reproduced or utilized in any form
or by any means, electronic or mechanical, including photocopying,
recording, or any information storage and retrieval system,
without permission in writing from the publisher.

First published in the United States, Great Britain, Canada,
Australia, and New Zealand in 1995 by North-South Books,
an imprint of Nord-Süd Verlag AG, Gossau Zürich, Switzerland.
First paperback edition published in 1996.
Distributed in the United States by North-South Books Inc., New York.

Library of Congress Cataloging-in-Publication Data
Wagener, Gerda.
[Fetzer jagt die Maus. English]
A mouse in the house! / by Gerda Wagener ; illustrated by Uli Waas.
Summary: A family tries to protect a mouse from its pet cat.
[1. Mice—Fiction. 2. Cats—Fiction. 3. Family life—Fiction.]
I. Waas, Uli, ill. II. Lanning, Rosemary. III. Title.
PZ7.W123Mo 1995
[E]—dc20 95-8453
A CIP catalogue record for this book is available
from The British Library.

For more information about our books,
and the authors and artists who create them, visit our web site:
http://www.northsouth.com

ISBN 1-55858-506-0 (TRADE BINDING)
1 3 5 7 9 TB 10 8 6 4 2
ISBN 1-55858-507-9 (LIBRARY BINDING)
1 3 5 7 9 LB 10 8 6 4 2
ISBN 1-55858-621-0 (PAPERBACK)
1 3 5 7 9 PB 10 8 6 4 2
Printed in Belgium

My name is Julia, and I have a cat. He
is called Socks, because of his white paws.
This is me, holding him. And that's my
brother Martin and my little sister Katie.

Katie always says Socks belongs to her, but that's not true. He was my cat before she was even born! Most of the time Socks curls up on the rocking chair and goes to sleep. I wish he would play with us more, like he used to.

Mother says, "He's not as young as he was." But that doesn't stop him from getting into trouble. Like he did a few days ago, for instance. Here is what happened:

Katie suddenly screamed, "Help! Socks caught something!"

I ran into the living room. Socks was crouching under the bookcase. His eyes were glowing and his tail went *swish, swish* from side to side. He had a mouse in his mouth. A sweet little thing with shiny black eyes.

"Socks!" I yelled. "Let it go, now!"
Socks just growled. And he crawled
farther under the bookcase.

"He must have caught it in the garden,"
said Martin. "I saw him prowling around
under the apple tree."

Katie was lying on the floor, trying to get the mouse away from Socks. "Let the mouse go, Socks," she said. "Come on. Give it to me." She was almost crying, she was so upset.

Mother came out of her study. "What's going on?" she asked.

"Socks's got a mouse," I said.

"He must have caught it in the garden," said Martin.

"Oh my goodness!" said Mother. She tried to coax Socks out.

But would he come out? Of course not.
He just growled.

Mother clapped her hands. "Out you go,
Socks, into the garden!" she shouted.

"Give the mouse to me, Socks," wailed
Katie, reaching under the bookcase.

Then Socks decided he'd had enough.
He shot out from under the bookcase and
ran into the kitchen. We all ran after him.

"No, Socks!" screamed Mother. "Not in the kitchen, for heaven's sake!" She threw a cushion at him.

Socks was so shocked, he let go of the mouse. The mouse scuttled into the crack beside the stove.

"Oh, no," groaned Mother. "Now there's a mouse loose in the house. I can't move the stove to get him out."

Socks scampered across the kitchen, sniffing the floor.

Then he sat down in front of the stove.
Right next to the little crack the mouse
had run into.

"Socks, you are very, very bad!" said Katie, and she tried to carry him away.

Socks scrabbled to get free, and he scratched her on the arm.

"Let him go," said Mother. "Socks isn't really bad. Animals aren't good or bad, like people. They just do what their instinct tells them."

"But he shouldn't eat the poor mouse," said Katie.

"Don't worry, Katie," said Mother. "That mouse isn't going to let Socks catch him again." She went back to her study.

"Come on, Katie," I said. "We'll try to get Socks to come into the living room."

First we rustled Mother's newspaper. Socks loves to tear up newspapers.

But Socks wouldn't come.

Then we crumpled paper into balls and threw them across the floor for him to chase.

Socks still wouldn't come. So we tried rattling the tin we keep the treats in. But Socks stayed stubbornly in the kitchen.

So we gave up.

"We'd better catch the mouse before Socks does," said Martin. "We could build a trap with a net. It wouldn't hurt the mouse."

I knew what he meant. We'd all seen a show on TV about scientists in Africa who caught a lion. They took a good look at him and then let him go.

"Okay," I said. "We'll build it in your room."

I went and got a net. We built a wall,
using all Martin's building blocks and
some of mine. It was a pretty big trap.

"Now we have to stretch the net
across," I said.

"You hold that side," said Martin, "and
I'll pull."

But the net was too small. It pulled the
walls down, and all the blocks clattered
onto the floor.

Mother heard the noise and came running.

"*Now* what's going on?" she said, and sighed.

We explained that we were trying to build a sort of African trap. "Like on TV," said Martin.

"But the net was too small," I said.

"The mouse! The mouse!" shrieked Katie.

Martin and I ran into the living room. Mother was close behind us.

"It ran right across the room," said Katie breathlessly, "but it looked happy."

"Oh, great," said Mother. "There's a jungle trap in the bedroom. The living room is a mess. But never mind. At least the mouse is happy."

She picked up the newspapers and all the rest of the stuff we had left on the living room floor. But there were big creases between her eyebrows. When Mother frowns like that, the best thing to do is disappear. We went into my room and shut the door. Socks scratched at the door, but we wouldn't let him come in. We didn't want him to hear what we were saying.

We crawled under the table to talk
things over.

"We ought to give the mouse a name,"
I said.

Martin suggested Hercules.

Katie said no, we had to call it Lisa.
That's the name of her best friend at
nursery school.

"All right, it's Lisa," I said. "Because
Katie saw the mouse first."

"We must try to save Lisa," I told the others.

"You're right," said Martin. "But how?"

We talked and argued for a long time. Then we agreed to put some food in a secret place in every room, so Lisa wouldn't starve to death. We could use leftovers from our school lunch boxes.

Katie painted a picture and we hung it on Socks's basket. She asked me to write "NO!" on it, in big letters, but I'm not sure that Socks really understood what it meant.

Over the next few days Socks and Lisa kept us very busy. Mother bought a trap to catch Lisa without hurting her. Every day, we moved it to a different place.

That's because Lisa ran all around the house. Martin and I could see where she had been when we looked at our secret food supplies. One day the salami disappeared from behind the kitchen cupboard. The next day the chocolate was gone from the bathroom. We didn't tell Mother. She wouldn't have been pleased to hear we were feeding Lisa.

Socks seemed to have forgotten about Lisa. He just lay in the rocking chair, dozing. His nose sometimes twitched, though, as if he could still smell her.

Lisa was starting to be a nuisance. Mother went to peel the carrots and found tooth marks in them. And there were little mouse droppings all over the place.

One day Lisa even ran across a picture
Katie had just painted. The paint was still
wet, and you could see the little footprints
quite clearly. Katie was very proud of that
picture, but Mother wouldn't let her take
it to nursery school.

"What would the other mothers think?"
she said.

I think she's embarrassed that we've got
a mouse in the house, even though it was
Socks's fault.

Then Lisa chewed a corner of my reading book. Mother had to let me take the book back to school. So now, at last, the other kids in my class were going to believe what I'd told them about our mouse.

That afternoon Simon and Freddie came over.

"May we look at your mouse?" Simon asked.

Mother laughed. Maybe she didn't really mind people knowing about Lisa after all.

"You can look," she said, "but the mouse may not let you see her."

She was right. Lisa had decided to stay out of sight. We looked under all the beds and cupboards and chests of drawers, but there was no sign of her. We did find twenty-five mouse droppings, though, and bits of food that had been nibbled.

Simon and Freddie thought we were so lucky to have Lisa. They had never had a mouse in their house. Martin said, "Let's hold a mousetrap competition. Whoever makes the best trap wins the prize."

Then Katie burst into my room, holding Mother's trap on her head. "Look, here's Lisa!" she said.

Simon and Freddie were really impressed. Martin got a piece of cheese from the refrigerator. But Lisa wasn't hungry. Maybe she was too scared to eat with so many people staring at her. So I decided that only Martin and I were allowed to hold the cage.

Katie started to cry, and Simon said that Lisa was probably just as scared of Martin and me as she was of anyone else.

"No she isn't!" I said.

"Yes she is," shouted Simon and Freddie and Katie.

"Ha!" I said. "What do you know about it? You've never had a mouse!"

Mother heard the shouting and came in. She took the trap away from us and put it on top of the bookshelf, out of reach, until we'd all calmed down.

Lisa was running up and down, looking nervous.

"Well, I'm glad we've caught Lisa at last," said Mother. "Now let's take her into the garden and set her free."

"No! I want to keep her," said Martin. "She can live in my room, in a cage."

"Oh, no she can't," said Mother.

"Can I take her home with me?" asked Freddie. "My mother really likes mice."

"No," she said. "Lisa is used to living out in the open."

"But if we set her free in the garden," I said, "Socks might catch her again. And then he'll eat her."

Mother nodded. "We'd better take her farther away than that," she said.

We went into the hall and put on our coats. Katie insisted on bringing her doll's blanket, to keep Lisa warm.

Then suddenly we heard a terrible noise from my room.

We ran in and saw the trap lying on the floor. Socks had knocked it off the bookcase. He was trying to pull Lisa out of the trap!

"Socks!" I shouted. "Get out of here!" But he wouldn't go, and he scratched me when I tried to pick up the trap.

"We really must get that mouse out of the house," said Mother.

We headed down to the woods. I was carrying the trap to begin with. But I'd only gone about ten steps when Katie wanted to hold it. Then Simon. And then Freddie. Everyone had a turn carrying Lisa.

In the woods Mother found a soft cushion of moss and put the trap down very gently. She opened the little door and Lisa ran out, fast as lightning, and disappeared into the bushes.

"Bye, Lisa!" called Katie. Mother put a little apple under the bush for Lisa, and Katie put two pieces of chocolate next to it. Then we walked slowly home.

"I'm going to miss Lisa," I said.

"Me too," said Martin. "She was a nice little mouse."

"We can come and visit her sometimes, can't we?" asked Katie.

"Yes," said Martin. "Let's do that."

"And could we buy a toy mouse for Socks?" I asked Mother.

"We'll do that first thing tomorrow," she said with a smile.

ABOUT THE AUTHOR

GERDA WAGENER was born in Sauerland, a pretty, mountainous area of Germany. She studied sociology and German language and literature, and worked first as a private tutor, then as a social worker. However, she much prefers writing poetry and children's books.

Ms. Wagener has lived in Wuppertal, Germany, for many years. Her house has a garden with a lime tree and columbines, and she has a black cat called Makki who sometimes brings a mouse into the house.

ABOUT THE ILLUSTRATOR

ULI WAAS was born in Donauworth, Bavaria. She studied painting and graphic design at the Academy of Art in Munich. She has illustrated a number of books for children, including two other easy-to-read books for North-South: *Where's Molly?* and *Spiny*. She particularly likes stories about children and animals. Uli Waas lives with her husband and their daughter and son on the edge of the Swabian Alps, where there are hundreds of cats and mice.

NORTH-SOUTH EASY-TO-READ BOOKS

Loretta and the Little Fairy
by Gerda Marie Scheidl, illustrated by Christa Unzner-Fischer

Little Polar Bear and the Brave Little Hare
by Hans de Beer

Where's Molly?
by Uli Waas

The Extraordinary Adventures of an Ordinary Hat
by Wolfram Hänel, illustrated by Christa Unzner-Fischer

Mia the Beach Cat
by Wolfram Hänel, illustrated by Kirsten Höecker

Lila's Little Dinosaur
by Wolfram Hänel, illustrated by Alex de Wolf

Meet the Molesons
by Burny Bos, illustrated by Hans de Beer

More from the Molesons
by Burny Bos, illustrated by Hans de Beer

On the Road with Poppa Whopper
*by Marianne Busser and Ron Schröder,
illustrated by Hans de Beer*

Spiny
by Jürgen Lassig, illustrated by Uli Waas

Rinaldo, the Sly Fox
by Ursel Scheffler, illustrated by Iskender Gider

The Return of Rinaldo, the Sly Fox
by Ursel Scheffler, illustrated by Iskender Gider

Rinaldo on the Run
by Ursel Scheffler, illustrated by Iskender Gider